PUG

I Like to Read® books, created by award-winning
picture book artists as well as talented newcomers,
instill confidence and the joy of reading in new readers.

We want to hear every new reader say, "I like to read!"

PUG

by Ethan Long

I Like to Read®

HOLIDAY HOUSE • NEW YORK

Pug sees Peg.

Pug sees Mom.

Yap Yap Yap

Pug sees Dad.

Pug sees Tad.

Tad sees Pug.

Pug wants to go.

No, Pug, no.

Go, Pug, go.

No Peg.

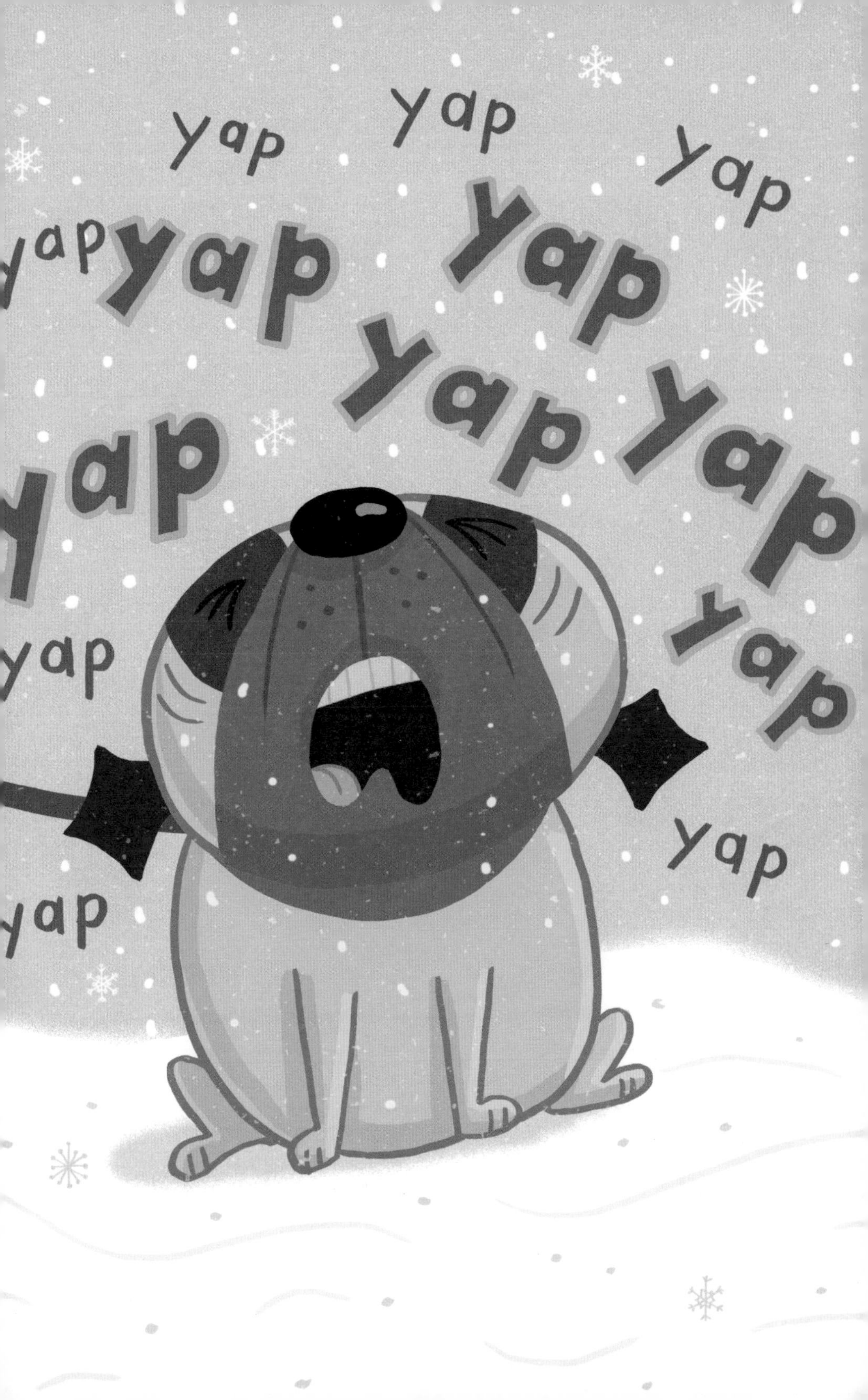
yap
yap
yap
yap
yap
yap
yap
yap
yap

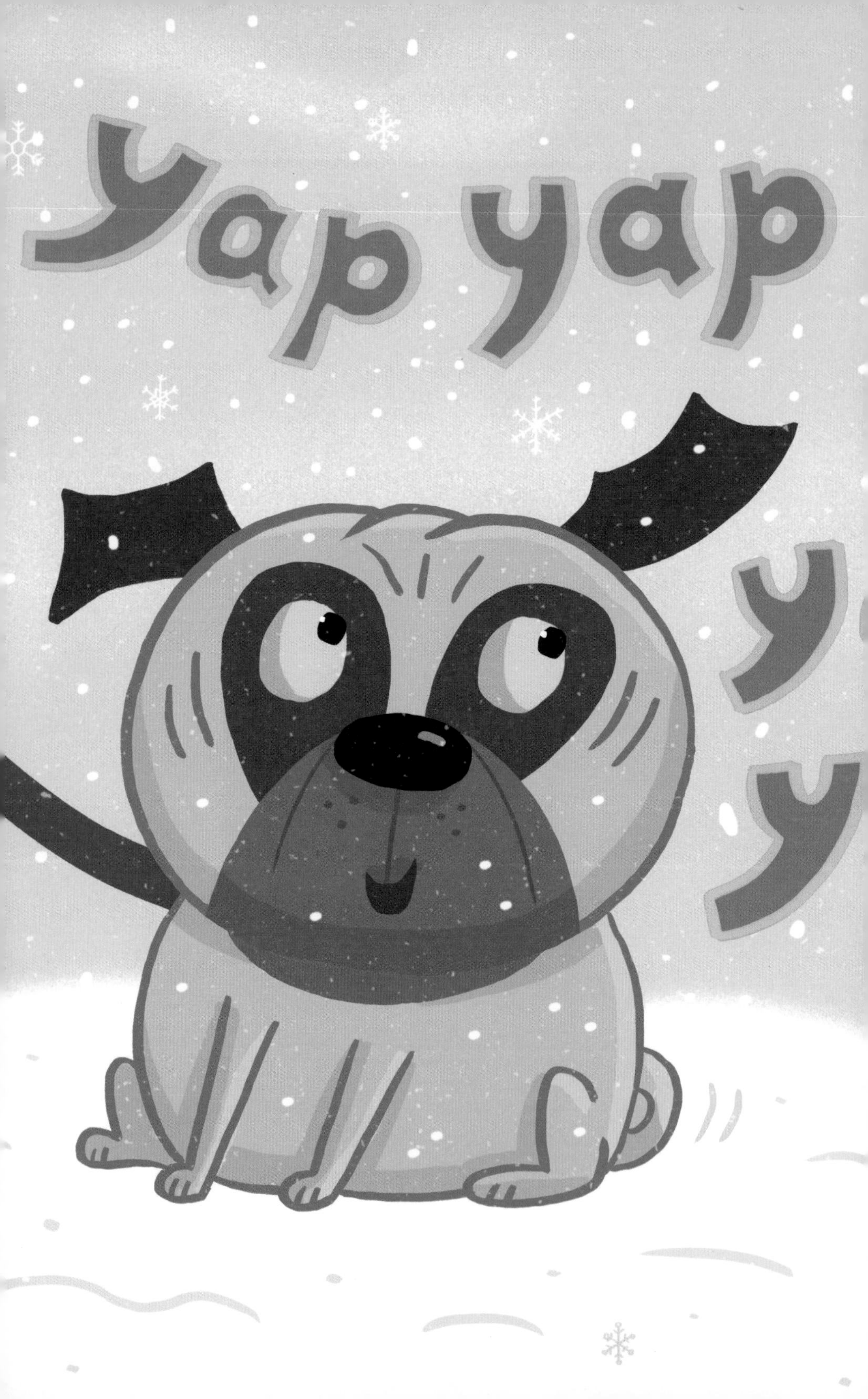
Yap yap

yap yap
yap yap yap
yap yap yap
yap

Pug sees Peg.

I LIKE TO READ is a registered trademark of Holiday House Publishing, Inc.
Copyright © 2016 by Ethan Long
All Rights Reserved
HOLIDAY HOUSE is registered in the U.S. Patent and Trademark Office.
Printed and bound in September 2018 at Hong Kong Graphics and Printing Ltd., China.
The artwork was created digitally.
www.holidayhouse.com
3 5 7 9 10 8 6 4 2

Library of Congress Cataloging-in-Publication Data
Names: Long, Ethan, author, illustrator.
Title: Pug / by Ethan Long.
Description: First Edition. | New York : Holiday House, [2016] | Series: I
like to read | Summary: "After seeing his friend Peg getting a walk
outside in the snow Pug must be persistent to convince his teenaged master
to take him out for a walk as well"— Provided by publisher.
Identifiers: LCCN 2015040852 | ISBN 9780823436453 (hardcover)
Subjects: LCSH: Pug—Fiction. | Dogs—Fiction. | CYAC: Dog walking—Fiction.
Classification: LCC PZ7.L8453 Pu 2016 | DDC [E]—dc23 LC record available at http://lccn.loc.gov/2015040852

ISBN 978-0-8234-3688-0 (paperback)
ISBN 978-0-8234-3989-8 (6 x 9 paperback)

I Like to Read®

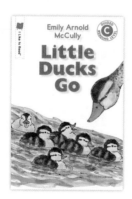